Who Owns Kelly Paddik?

Beth Goobie

orca soundings

ORCA BOOK PUBLISHERS

Library and Archives Canada Cataloguing in Publication

Goobie, Beth, 1959—
Who owns Kelly Paddik? / Beth Goobie

(Orca soundings)
ISBN 1-55143-239-0

I. Title. II. Series.

PS8563.O8326W56 2003   jC813'.54   C2002-911413-6
PZ7.G597Wh 2003

Summary: After attempting suicide, Kelly Paddik is sent to a "secure facility." As she tries to find a way out she has to come to terms with her memories of abuse.

First published in the United States, 2003
Library of Congress Control Number: 2002115795

Orca Book Publishers gratefully acknowledges the support for its publishing programs provided by the following agencies: the Government of Canada through the Book Publishing Industry Development Program and the Canada Council for the Arts, and the Province of British Columbia through the BC Arts Council and the Book Publishing Tax Credit.

Cover design: Christine Toller
Cover image: Eyewire

In Canada: In the United States:
Orca Book Publishers   Orca Book Publishers
Box 5626 Stn. B   PO Box 468
Victoria, BC Canada   Custer, WA USA
V8R 6S4   98240-0468

www.orcabook.com
08 07 06 • 5 4 3
Printed and bound in Canada.

*for the young women
who spend a time at Marymound*
BG

Chapter One

I sat in the car next to my social worker and stared out the window. We were out of the downtown area now, driving up Main Street into Winnipeg's north end. The car passed store after store, then a McDonald's. A woman at a bus stop stared straight at me, then looked away with nothing on her face. That was what it was like when you were a kid in the system. So many people looking right through you with polite nothingness on their faces. It always made me wonder if the nothingness came from them or me.

I'm fifteen years old and I'm being driven to a lockup. The thought kept pounding through my head. Outside the car, yellow leaves blew down the street like sadness, like freedom. The car turned off Main Street and passed a row of houses. At the end of the street stood a huge black iron gate. It was like something out of a horror movie. The car drove through the gate into a parking lot. Ahead of us was a tall, very old brick building. The sign out front said: MARYMOUND SCHOOL FOR GIRLS.

Two days ago I'd been here for a meeting, but this time I was here to stay. As the car got close to the front door, I saw the wires in the windows. Wire run through glass makes windows harder to smash and climb out. That means you can't get out — you're stuck wherever you are until someone decides to let you out.

I wasn't even inside yet, and I could feel the walls moving in on me. Waves of panic rose up my throat, and I felt as if I was drowning. I couldn't let them do this to me, *I couldn't*.

Pushing open the car door, I dug my feet into the ground and took off for the gate. I could hear my social worker yelling, but then a huge roaring filled my ears. At the parking lot entrance, the horror movie gate still stood open, waiting for me.

I had to get away — that was all I could think about. The gate grew and grew, and then I was through it and out in the street. Everything in me pulled together and began to run, as fast as my heart was beating, faster.

Then I heard feet pounding after me. They were gorilla feet — loud and heavy. I didn't have to look back to know they were a man's. He was right behind me, and I gave up then because men are stronger and meaner than girls. I know that if I know anything. I stopped running and felt the air stand still around me. I was gasping, trying to catch my breath as I watched the street run away without me. The man's hand touched my arm — not too heavy, but there.

"I'll give you a minute to catch your breath," he said.

I didn't say anything. He stood there panting, waiting for me to stop breathing so hard. I wouldn't look at him, just stared down the street and pretended his hand wasn't on my arm. Finally he said, "Kelly, I'm Jim. I think we'll head back now."

We walked back in silence. I kept kicking

at leaves and watching my feet. *Prisoner feet*, I thought as we walked through the gate. When we got to the car, my social worker glared at me.

"That wasn't very smart, Kelly Paddik."

I tried to look at her as if I'd never seen her before and couldn't care less. Inside, though, I was crying — crying in my hands and stomach and legs.

I looked away from my social worker's face, and then I saw the woman standing beside her. Even though she wasn't wearing a headdress, I could tell right away that she was a nun. Her uniform was a light brown, and there was a small cross on her chest. Seeing a nun scared me so bad I thought my knees and elbows were going to come apart. It's just that in stories and movies there are always nuns in places like this. That's how you know you're locked up for good.

"Hello, Kelly. I'm Sister Mary." She was so short, the top of her head came to my shoulders. And she was old — grandmother old. If all the staff in here were like this, I could run away easy. This started to cheer me up, until I remembered Jim.

"C'mon in and I'll show you your room," Sister Mary said.

Just like hotel service, I thought.

Jim followed close behind to make sure I didn't make a run for it again. I felt as if I was wearing him like a body glove. He probably thought of himself as my bodyguard — just a nice guy keeping Kelly Paddik away from all the bad stuff. So if he was so nice, then why was he making my hands sweat and my heart pound? I wanted to turn around and shove him, hard.

Before I could, Sister Mary opened the front door and we stepped inside the building. It seemed very dark after the bright sunshine and the yellow flyaway leaves. From somewhere nearby, I could hear girls' voices. We went down a long hall and through a locked door. Then we climbed two flights of stairs. I was watching the old nun, waiting to see if she would fall over from all this exercise. But she wasn't even breathing hard. Maybe she worked out and lifted weights.

When we got to the top of the stairs, we turned down another hall. On my left I could see an office with a large window run through with wire. I guess the staff thought they needed somewhere safe to hide out. Ahead of us there was a big room with sofas, a TV, and a kitchen area. On both sides of this room were five doors. *One girl per room*, I thought. *That makes ten girls.*

Sister Mary led me to the middle door on the left. She unlocked the door and said, "The girls in this unit are twelve to seventeen years old, Kelly. I'm the supervisor. Anytime you want to talk to me about anything, just let one of the staff know. This is your room."

I walked into the narrow room after her, followed by Jim. It really was small — one sneeze would fill the place right up. Honestly, four or five steps would take you across it. And there was no place to hide anything, unless you stuck it in the heating vent. As I thought about this, Jim put my suitcase on the bed. Then he opened it and started going through my stuff. I could feel my anger rising in a huge wave. But I got it under control. You have to do that in these places — sit tight on everything you feel. If you don't, you lose it and you're locked up longer. I always sit tight on my anger and sadness and don't let any of it show. It ends up feeling as if I'm sitting on myself — as if I've got this big bum parked on my head. But if it means I'll get out faster, that's all that matters.

"I don't have a bomb in there," I muttered.

"I'm sorry, Kelly. We have to do this," Jim said. Then he held up my pet rock. It was a hunk of granite I'd picked up off a beach somewhere and decided to love. Stupid, I know. I called it "Family" and talked to it when no one else was around. My pet rock was a great listener. At least it never interrupted.

"We're going to have to keep this in the office," said Jim.

"But that's my pet rock. I need it in my room with me," I said.

Jim shook his head. "It's one of the rules. You can't keep anything that could be used as a weapon in your room."

"But it's *a pet* rock, not a *killer* rock," I argued. I needed that rock. I told it everything.

"Sorry, Kelly. You'll get it back when you leave. Why don't you unpack now?" said Jim. Then he and Sister Mary left to go talk to my social worker.

I stood looking at the room they'd given me. There was hardly any furniture — just a dresser, a desk, and a bed. Then I saw the window, with wires run through it like all the others.

I leaned my face against the cool glass and stared out. I started to get cross-eyed staring at the wires. Outside, I could see a long hall that connected this building to a school. That had to be the way the girls got to classes. Beyond the school was a huge, fenced-in yard. *They don't even let you out when you go to school*, I thought.

I'd never believed this could happen to me — that I'd get locked up. I'd always wanted to be a normal kid in a normal family like everyone else. Somehow I'd gotten trapped in a life I didn't want. How had it turned out like this? How had I gotten to be some freak that they had to lock up?

I sat down on the bed next to my suitcase. The one thing I was glad about was that it was October. That meant I could wear long sleeves and no one could see the skin on my arm. Last week I'd cut my left wrist with broken glass. I was living in a group home then, where it's easier to get hold of what you need. I'd stolen a Coke from a staff person and smashed the bottle. I'd wanted everything to end then, but I'd messed up. So here I was, alive and locked up.

When the staff took me to the hospital, they told me that I was a "danger to myself and to others." Then they told me they were sending me to a place with more staff to help me work things out. That's the big sob story about how I got here, with wires on my window and a suitcase to unpack.

I stared at the stuff in my suitcase. I could feel Jim's fingerprints all over it. In fact, I felt as if his fingerprints were crawling all over *me*. Slowly I took out my socks and underwear and put them in the dresser. The most important stuff I didn't unpack, because you couldn't see it. That was the stuff I kept deep inside me. Only my pet rock heard about those secrets. I'd had them for as long as I could remember — memories of home, things my dad did to me at night when Mom was asleep.

I worked so hard, all the time, to forget those things. Those memories made my body feel thick, heavy and hard to move. When I thought about what went on at home, I got so scared I couldn't breathe. Sometimes, if I made myself move or run fast, I could get away from it for a while. When I was a little kid, I used to play a game. I would start at one end of the street and run until I was tired. I would pretend I could go so fast I could leave everything bad behind me. Like a small bird, I would fly up and away from my body forever. Too bad forever doesn't last very long.

In here, in this place, there was nowhere to run. I stood at my window and watched yellow leaves blow through the huge iron gate and out into the street. The leaves blurred together as the tears started. *Don't cry, Kelly*, I told myself. *It doesn't help, so don't bother. Just figure out how to get out of this place as fast as you can.*

Chapter Two

I decided that the first chance I had, I would take off. In the meantime, things would go easier if I pretended that I wanted to be here. So I hung my shirts and jeans in the closet, then looked at the last few things in my suitcase. On the top of a small pile sat an envelope with pictures of my family in it. I hadn't looked at them in a long time. Underneath were some notebooks full of writing.

I started to write stories when I was about five years old. When I was seven I decided to write the story of my life, but I didn't get very far. One of the oldest notebooks started off with: *I am seven. My mom and dad is big. J and D is smal.* That was about as much as I wanted to say, I guess.

"J" and "D" are Jolyn and Danny, my sister and brother. I hadn't seen or talked to them in years, but I thought about them a lot. The last time I saw Jolyn, she was hiding her teeth under her pillow for the tooth fairy. Danny was in diapers. Were they both still living with my mom? Or did they turn out like me and end up in a group home?

I'd written lots of other stories too, about good kids with happy lives. Those stories went on for pages and pages. It was easy to write stories like that. I could pretend that I was one of those kids. It was a little like looking out a window onto another life. I could get out of mine for a bit, and forget who I really was.

Suddenly I heard a lot of voices and footsteps out in the room with the TV. Since it was around three o'clock, I figured it must be the girls getting back from school. Quickly I shoved my notebooks into a dresser drawer. Then I sat on the bed and counted heartbeats.

"Hey, the new girl's here," someone called.

My doorway filled with faces, though none of the girls came into my room. My eyes kept wanting to lock onto the walls, but I made myself turn and look at the girls. Girls in lockups are supposed to be tougher than those in group homes. I tried to look as if lockups were nothing, as if I spent holidays in them.

"So, what's your name?" someone asked.

"Kelly." The word kind of flopped out of my mouth. *Great, advertise your nerves*, I thought. "What's yours?" I asked.

The girl asking the questions didn't answer. I guess she figured that wasn't her job. "What are you in here for?" she asked.

I could tell that she was the girl who ran this unit. There's always one who's tougher than everyone else. If you let her know you're scared, she'll ride you. So I shrugged and said, "Beats me. My social worker's in the office. Ask her."

I didn't want to tell the world about my arm. That was my business. But if I didn't give this girl an answer, it could mean trouble later on. She was already looking at me sideways, her lip curled like a pit bull's. I could see her getting ready to fire another question, but then a loud voice spoke up behind her.

"C'mon, ladies, break it up. Let Kelly get used to the place before you all jump on her."

One by one the girls backed away, leaving a woman standing in the doorway. She had a lot of red curly hair that could have spent some time with a comb. And she looked like she could run — not your grandmotherly type. "All right if I come in?" she asked.

I shrugged. What was I supposed to say? *No?*

Leaning against the dresser, she said, "I'm Fran. Welcome to Sister Mary's unit."

So that little nun did actually run this place. I tried not to look surprised. "Yeah, sure," I said.

She raised an eyebrow. Girls probably talked to her like this all day long. Lifting her hands, she ran them through her rebel hair. "How about if I ask one of the girls to show you around and explain the rules?"

"Yeah, sure." I shrugged again. This place wasn't anything to get excited about. On the other hand, I did need to know how to get to the washroom.

Going to the door, Fran called out, "Chris."

I held my breath, hoping it wasn't the girl

who'd asked all the questions. But the face that showed up had on a grin that looked as if it belonged there. Her black hair was cut short and her eyes were really dark. She was cool, but not a staff kind of cool, as in *I'll like you as long as you do what you're told.* Chris told me that she was Cree and came from a place up north called Churchill.

"Ever seen a polar bear?" I asked.

"Sure. Have you?" She looked at me kind of strange when she said this. I realized that asking if someone has seen a polar bear isn't usually the first question you ask a stranger. So I pulled out the last thing in my suitcase and handed it to her. It was a grubby, falling-apart white bear. Every girl in a group home has a couple of stuffed animals on her bed — something from home. They always look like they've been through a war.

When she saw it, Chris laughed again. Her laugh was kind of tricky. It got inside you and then you were smiling without even realizing it. I guess the building looked so old and creepy, I didn't think anyone would be laughing in here. It made me wonder why Chris was here if she could laugh like that.

Chris showed me around the unit and listed

off the bath rules, bedtime rules and snacktime rules. They sure had more rules in lockups than they did in group homes. I followed her around, waiting for the rules about blowing your nose and tying your shoes.

Chris was showing me the kitchen seating plan when I saw Fran go into the washroom. Suddenly I heard Fran call out, "Who's the drip that left the tap on?"

Chris burst out laughing. "Ever sick!" she called back.

Fran's head popped out the washroom door. "D'you know what I mean, or d'you know what I mean?" she sang out.

I rolled my eyes. Dumb jokes always had me wanting to crawl into the nearest grave. Suddenly I realized someone was standing behind me, so close that I could feel her body heat. Turning quickly, I saw the girl who ran this unit, the one who'd asked me all those questions. *Pit Bull*, I thought. Why was she so interested in the back of my neck?

"What's so funny?" Pit Bull asked. Her lips were faking a smile, but her eyes wouldn't have fooled anyone.

"Ah, you know Fran — always joking

around," said Chris. She lost her grin and a new kind of cool came into her face — the kind that puts you into deep freeze. Chris didn't fake things, and she didn't like Pit Bull. "I've got to go talk to someone. See you, Kelly." She walked away.

I decided the best thing to do was stare out a nearby window. It was either that window or a wall — the last thing I wanted to look at was Pit Bull's face. Things got real quiet beside me, but I knew she was still there. Finally I gave up and snuck a glance at her. She was staring right at me.

"I'm Terri," she said.

Her eyes were that pale kind of blue that looks like the sky died in them. She'd squinted them into tough little slits. With a lot of black eyeliner around them, they could really nail you to a wall. Right away she started firing more questions at me.

"So, where'd you live before here?"

I pulled down the edge of my sleeve, even though it was long enough to cover the stitches on my left arm. "Siberia," I said.

"No, seriously." Her voice giggled, but her eyes kept shoving me against the wall.

Sweet'n'sour, I thought. "In a group home," I said.

"Which school did you go to?" she asked.

"Why?" I asked, staring out the window.

"Just wondering if you know any of my friends," she said.

I doubt it, I wanted to say, but the fact was that I probably did know them. Everyone knew them. They were the kind of girls most people spent their time trying to forget. I decided this was probably a wise moment to change the subject. "So, what d'you do here for fun after supper?" I asked.

"Rollerskating." Pit Bull shrugged. "I know, it's kid stuff, but it's something to do. You any good at rollerskating?"

"I'm okay," I said carefully.

Her pale blue eyes zoned right in on me. "You suck up to staff?"

"No!" I knew right then that I was going to have to stop talking to Chris. She was nice, but she was too friendly with the staff, and that didn't go well with Pit Bull. I didn't like Pit Bull, but I knew how these places worked. I'd had one little chat with Chris, and already trouble was breathing down my neck. I didn't want trouble, I just wanted out of here.

Pit Bull started to nail me with another

question just as Fran came out of the washroom. She was picking at her teeth with a paperclip.

"Hey, Terri — why don't you help me unload supper from the dumb waiter?" she asked. Looking right at me, Pit Bull let a smile ooze across her face. Then she linked her arm with Fran's and walked away. *What a fake*, I thought. *Talk about sucking up.*

I went back to my room and stared out my window. Every time I moved into a new place, there were so many new people — new girls, new staff. None of them ever meant anything, and nothing ever changed. I just kept moving from place to place and meeting more strangers. Who cared about any of them? I leaned against my window and tried to stare past the thoughts that were whirling inside my head. I had to keep looking at what was out there, outside myself, where it was safe. If I didn't, I would start to see what was hidden inside me. I tried never to see those things, but I knew they were there, just waiting for me to remember them.

I could feel that big bum again, sitting on my head. *Get me out of here*, I kept thinking. *Out of this place. Out of my life.*

Chapter Three

When I checked the seating plan at supper, I found out that Chris sat at my table. Another girl named Ellen also sat with us, but she was pretty quiet and didn't say much. After filling her plate with chili, Fran joined us. I could see Pit Bull at the next table, her eyes glued to the side of my head.

Chris and Ellen started talking about winning the lottery. Whether you live free or locked up, you'll always find someone dreaming about winning the big one. Chris said, "I'd buy a jeep, but my granny says a car is a waste of money."

I'd get a car, I thought. *A fast car.*

Fran nodded. "I'm with your granny. I'd rather spend the money on a trip. I'd go to China."

Chris shrugged. "My granny would rather go to Bingo."

Fran got up for a second helping of chili. *Man*, I thought, *I hope she gets off before those beans start kicking in.* Out of the corner of my eye, I could see Pit Bull still watching me. That girl had rabies. "Pit Bull," I muttered, shifting my chair so I couldn't see her.

"Huh?" Chris asked, her mouth full. She looked at the way I was turned in my chair, then glanced around and saw Pit Bull. Suddenly she started to laugh so hard that everyone turned to stare at us.

"Do you mind?" I hissed at her. All I needed was Pit Bull thinking I was telling jokes about her behind her back.

With a shrug, Chris calmed down. "Pit Bull," she said, grinning. "That's great. You're a genius, Kelly."

Just then a beautiful voice came floating up the stairway. I recognized the tune right away. It was one of the old swing songs my mom liked, but I'd never heard anyone sing it like this.

"Sister Mary!" Chris yelled. Jumping up, she ran down the hallway to hug the nun. Since when did nuns hum big band songs?

Coming into the unit, Sister Mary sat down at our table and gave me a grin. "I just came up to see how Kelly was doing. How's the supper, ladies? I made the chili."

Girls were crowding around our table. Smiles were everywhere, even on Pit Bull's face. Sister Mary seemed pretty popular. "I've got something for you, Kelly," she said and handed me a rolled-up poster.

"Sister Mary gives everyone a poster when they come here," Chris said. "C'mon, open it."

Everyone's eyes were on me as I unrolled the poster. It was a picture straight out of a dream — a huge sky with one seagull flying, bright white in the sun. But it was wrecked by the words that ran across the bottom: LOVE YOURSELF. *Yeah, right*, I thought, studying the poster. *Hand someone a pretty picture with a few dumb words on it, and all the problems are solved, right?* But I knew better than to say what I was thinking out loud. Faking my best smile, I said, "Thanks."

Sister Mary looked at me closely. I

wondered if she could see the little white bird inside me that wanted to fly out and away. But all she did was smile and stand up. "Is everyone ready for rollerskating?" she asked.

I rolled up the poster and put it in my room. No way was I putting something that corny on my wall. Out in the unit the girls were getting ready to head to the gym for rollerskating. As we started down the stairs, I saw girls from the other two units ahead of us. Beside me walked Chris, grinning her head off. Every now and then she would glance at Pit Bull and laugh softly.

"How many girls are there in this place?" I asked her.

"Thirty. Ten in each unit." She pointed down a hall. "That's where the social workers' offices are."

Oh great, I thought. *Social workers two floors down.* We reached the bottom of the stairs and turned into a hallway — the long hall I'd seen from my bedroom window. Girls from the other units were watching me and whispering. I tried not to stare back. I could see Pit Bull close by, talking to girls from another unit. *Spreading the word about me*, I thought and watched my feet. The hallway seemed to go on forever.

Finally a staff unlocked a door at the other end and we passed through.

"That's the door to the school," Chris told me. "The gym's right here."

We got the skates from the equipment room and put them on. I could hardly wait to get onto the floor. When I was a kid, I took skating lessons. I even won a few contests. I figured I could blow Pit Bull's mind with my skating and then she would treat me differently. Maybe she would even decide to make me one of her friends. That would make life a lot easier in this place. As soon as I had my skates on I was off, skating as fast as I could. I went around and around that dinky old gym, doing all my best moves.

Sometimes skating works for me. The louder the music, the better. I ride the beat and when I'm moving fast on skates, I almost feel free. As I skated around the Marymound gym, I forgot Pit Bull and all her lousy questions. I kept going around and around, trying to work up more speed. My moves fit me like a glove, and my heavy ugly body felt beautiful. I could tell a lot of the girls were watching. When I passed Pit Bull, she looked away. She was impressed, I could tell.

I could see Chris over by the equipment room, still putting on her skates. If she didn't get on the floor soon, she was going to miss the whole evening. About my seventh time around the gym, I got tired and slowed down. I was doing circles, going into a back corner, when a group came up behind me. They swarmed me and someone shoved me.

"Pit Bull, eh?" a voice hissed.

My shirt tore, and I stumbled. I put out my hands, but the wall slammed into my shoulder. I think I hit my head — for a second everything went dark. Then the gym came back, but it was pretty quiet. Someone had shut off the music.

"Everyone off the floor," a staff called.

I was all right, but my shoulder ached and my head hurt. As I turned, three girls skated away from me. Pit Bull was one of them. Breathing hard, I rested against the wall. Fran skated up.

"Everything all right?" she asked.

"Yeah, sure," I said.

"C'mon over to the equipment room," she said.

I followed her, saying, "I'm all right, I'm all right." Another staff called Pit Bull and her friends to the equipment room. As Fran and I

25

skated up to them, my body felt heavy and fat again. I stared at my feet. Someone put the music back on and the other girls started skating. But they were watching me — everyone was watching.

Pit Bull put on big innocent eyes, blinked them a lot and said, "It was an accident!" Then she looked at me and said, "Right, Kelly?" She didn't wait for my answer. "We just wanted to talk to her, but we got going too fast and bumped into her."

"Is that right, Kelly?" Fran asked.

"Sure." I wanted this to be over. Pit Bull ran these girls. It was obvious that she'd told one of her friends to shove me into the wall. I was lucky, really. It could have been a lot worse. If I complained now, who knew what would happen next time? Besides, I didn't like all these people watching me. I wanted to get some space. Then I saw Pit Bull's eyes slide down my left arm. I followed her gaze and felt sick. So that was what tore when I was pushed. My left sleeve was ripped. Everyone could see the stitches in my arm. Slowly I pulled one of the torn ends over the cut. *No matter how bad things get*, I thought, *they can always get worse.*

"Since you can't control yourselves, you

three ladies are off the floor for the evening," Fran said, sounding angry. "C'mon — off with the skates."

After Pit Bull and her friends took off their skates, they left the gym with one of the staff. *Great,* I thought. *Now Pit Bull has another reason to get mad at me.* She must have heard Chris giggling about the nickname. Chris was definitely someone I needed to stay away from. Going to the opposite end of the gym, I sat down. I was finished with skating for the evening. All I wanted was for it to end so that I could go back to my room. As I started unlacing my skates, someone sat down beside me.

"Get lost," I said, without looking up. I meant it too. I was ready to haul off and shove anyone who came too close.

"When Terri does stuff like that to me, I feel like I'm outside." It was Chris, talking so softly that I could hardly hear her. What was her problem? Couldn't she take a hint, or didn't people from Churchill know how to do that? I stared at the skaters, but she kept right on talking. "I feel outside," she said, "like I'm on the road, out in the cold. Like no one will take me. Like I've got no family."

I shot Chris a sideways glance. Her face looked as sad as an old story, and she kept twisting her hands. Why didn't she just shut up and go away? This wasn't her problem.

"Terri makes me feel as if I can't be who I want to be," she said, glancing at me.

So what? I wanted to say. I didn't like talking about sad stuff, and I sure didn't want to hear about anyone else's problems. I had enough of my own to keep me busy, thank you. I started snapping my fingers to the music. "Can't let it get to you." I shrugged.

"It gets to me," Chris said, watching the skaters. "Does your arm get itchy? Y'know — when it's getting better?"

"I guess." My arm hadn't had time to get better yet. But then, nothing in my life had ever gotten better.

"I don't like skating night." Chris laughed, her voice high and nervous. "Too many people. I'm not a very good skater."

I finally had to smile. Here was Chris, sitting in a back corner of the gym, keeping an eye on the new girl. She wasn't dumping her problems on me, she was just trying to make me feel better. And her words were real, not just some dumb saying on a poster.

"C'mon," I said. "I can show you some moves if you want. It's easy, once you get going. And now that Pit Bull's gone, we'll have lots of room to move around."

Chapter Four

That night I lay awake for a long time, holding my stuffed bear and staring out the window. On the other side of the wire, the tiny moon looked far away. In my last group home I used to lie in bed and pretend that I could fly to the moon. Like some thin white bird, I would fly up and away, leaving my body behind on the bed. With all that wire crisscrossed over the moon, though, it was hard to pretend. I hate crying. My pillow gets soaked. My nose feels thick as a tree trunk, and

I think I'll never be able to breathe normally again. Why do you have to feel *and* look like crap at the same time?

My nose was back to normal by the time Fran stuck her head through my doorway in the morning. "Time to get up," she said cheerfully.

I opened one eye, then closed it. She had on a bright yellow shirt and a big smile. As usual, her curly red hair looked as if it had never met a comb.

"Don't you get enough of this place?" I groaned. "Are you always here?"

Fran laughed. "Nah, you just got lucky. Washroom's to your left, in case you forgot."

I dragged myself to the washroom and looked in the mirror. My hair looked just like Fran's. It's short and blond and usually looks like the morning after. I stuck it under a tap to calm it down.

Without looking up, I knew when Pit Bull came into the washroom. I could feel her standing there, just looking at me. I figured I couldn't let Pit Bull *think* she could scare me. Very slowly, I picked up my towel, walked up to her and looked her in the eye.

"Slasher, eh?" she said softly.

I felt my face heat up, but I kept looking her right in the eye.

"Okay, Terri and Kelly — let's get moving!" It was Fran. They watched you pretty close in this place, but for once it was a relief. Without saying anything, I walked around Pit Bull and straight to my room.

Before school, Fran called me into the office. As I came in I saw Pit Bull sitting on a small couch, staring at the wall. "Terri has something to say to you," Fran said.

Pit Bull cleared her throat. "I'm sorry I bumped into you and tore your shirt," she said politely to the wall. She didn't even look at me. I thought about letting her wait for the wall to give her an answer. But if I acted like that, I would never get out of this place.

"Yeah, sure," I said, just as politely, to the same wall.

Without looking at me, Pit Bull stood up and shoved a note at me. It was a written apology. "So, can I go now?" she asked, turning to Fran. "I did what you said."

Fran sighed. "Sure, Terri. Off you go." Leaning out the door, she called out, "Everyone ready for school?"

My first class was math. I sat by the window. *More wire between me and the sky*, I thought. Leaves blew past the window, blurring into a long yellow streak. I blinked quickly and everything sorted it-self out. *You're useless*, I thought to myself. *Crying will get you nowhere except stuck inside your crazy no-good head.*

There was a knock at the door and then Fran popped her head in. She whispered something to the teacher.

"Kelly, you've got a meeting with your social worker," the teacher told me.

Not another one, I thought, following Fran. Sometimes it seemed as if I was always talking to social workers and counselors, people asking me questions. And I'd get the feeling they all knew my secret. That was the worst feeling of all — when I thought they could read my mind. As we walked, my stomach started to hurt. Fran turned into the social workers' hallway and knocked on a door.

"C'mon in," said a man's voice. I went stiff. I always need extra time to get ready if I'm walking into a room with a man in it. I followed Fran through the door.

"Hello, Kelly," said the man at the desk. "Remember me? I'm Jim." He was the man who'd chased me down the street and taken my pet rock.

I sat down in one of the chairs and made myself look at him. "Oh yeah," I said.

A tiny smile picked up a corner of Jim's mouth. "How are things going?" he asked. "I hear you had a bit of a rough time last night in the gym."

"So?" I looked him right in the eye without blinking. If I thought of him as part of the wall — a part that talked — nothing he said would matter.

He was looking at me thoughtfully. "You think you're a tough kid, don't you, Kelly?"

"I'm not going to tell you what I think," I said.

It got so quiet that I could almost hear the thoughts in Jim's head. He had very large eyebrows that jumped around a lot, and he was half-bald. He looked all right, as if he could take a joke. I had to work hard to keep thinking of him as part of the wall.

Finally he said, "Thinking is the most private thing you can do."

That surprised me, but all I did was shrug and say, "I guess."

Jim talked about the different programs they ran at Marymound, and then he cleared his throat. I could tell that he was getting to the important stuff. Social workers don't like to come to the point right away. They try to make you relax first. That means you get to sit on pins and needles until they tell you the real reason you're in their office.

Jim smiled at me. "Last week, while you were in the hospital," he said, "I met with your mother."

So that was why we were having this meeting. Right away I wanted to ask about my sister and brother. But just thinking about them made me remember my dad. My stomach twisted itself into an ugly fist.

"You don't feel very comfortable around your mother, do you, Kelly?" asked Jim.

"I haven't seen her in years," I said.

"Would you like to meet her again?" Jim asked. "We could meet here in my office."

"No." I didn't want to talk to my mom. I never looked at the pictures I had of her in that envelope. I hated her. Even though I had some good memories, I still hated her. When I told her about the things that happened to me, the things my dad did to me, she called me a liar. She didn't believe me. How could she not believe me? She didn't try to stop any of it, so it kept happening. That was why I started to run away from home when I was ten. I met up with some people who got me into a lot of trouble, working the streets.

Jim knows, I thought. *He's read my mind. Now he's going to make me remember.* I looked away. *Think of him as the wall*, I reminded myself.

Jim cleared his throat again. "Your mother says she's tried to contact you, and you won't talk to her."

"That's right." I stared past him at the wall. As I did, the wall started to move around. I could see a face starting to take shape inside it — the eyes, nose and mouth. I knew that face.

"Do you want to talk about it?" Jim asked.

"No!" I said loudly.

"You don't think you could just sit here and let her talk to you?" Jim asked. "Just listen to her for a bit?"

The nightmare face was swelling up, taking over the whole wall. "No!" I repeated, louder this time. "I just want to get out of here."

I started to kick the chair leg. I couldn't

talk to my mom. She would want to talk about the past, and she'd make me remember. It was too awful to remember. I worked so hard to forget. I worked so hard to keep my dad small and in dark places inside me. Anything could remind me of what he did to me when I was little. There he was right now, stepping out of the wall and coming towards me. Seeing him again made me so scared that I started screaming. Jim's office faded away. Suddenly I was five years old and my dad was coming into my bedroom. He was going to do those things to me all over again, and I was too little to stop him. It hurt, it hurt worse than I could ever tell you.

Finally Jim's office came back again. Fran was holding my left arm. Jim was on the other side, holding that arm. There was blood on my stitches. I guess I'd tried to scratch the cut open again.

Fran took me to the nurse, who said that my arm just needed cleaning. None of the stitches had come out. Fran and Jim must have moved fast. The nurse put peroxide on my arm. As I watched her clean the cut, my arm seemed to leave my body and float beside me in the air. I can do this sometimes — turn parts of my body off or make them feel like someone else's body.

"I don't ever want to see my mom again," I said slowly to Fran. "Never again. You can't make me."

"Why, Kelly?" Fran asked. "Can you tell us why?"

Inside, my dad had shrunk down very small, so small that I couldn't feel him. But I knew he was there. He was always there.

"No." I shook my head and stared at the wall. "Never. I can handle it. I'll take care of everything myself."

Chapter Five

For the next few days, all I saw were doors and windows. It didn't take long to figure out that the wired-over windows were no way out. But I noticed that most of the doors were opened with the same key. Every teacher, social worker, nun and staff seemed to have one of those keys. That meant there were lots of them around, and all I needed was one.

The stitches in my left arm were no longer a secret. The nurse had wrapped my forearm in a white bandage. Twice a day, one of the staff would unwrap the bandage and clean the stitches. Every time I looked up, a girl seemed to be staring at my arm. Most of them had a scared look on their faces, but Pit Bull's friends laughed. When they did, I fixed my eyes on the nearest door and thought of taking off through it. Doors were pretty much taking over my mind — who opened and closed them, which key went where. Let those girls laugh. When I got out of this place, I wouldn't be taking any of them with me.

One day after school, Jim came and stood in my doorway. I'd been lying on my bed, watching the last of the yellow leaves blow past my window. If it had been Fran, I would have kept lying there. But Jim made me think of my dad, coming through my bedroom door when I was small. My heart started beating so hard that it hurt. Clenching my fists, I sat up.

"How are you doing these days, Kelly?" Jim asked.

"I don't have anything to say to you," I said, watching his feet. If you want to know which way a person is going to move, you always watch his feet.

There was a long pause, but Jim just kept

standing there. Finally I glanced at his face and said, "Don't you get the message? I'm telling you to get lost."

His heavy eyebrows went up a bit. "I hear you like writing stories," he said. "I'd like to read one, if you'd let me. I brought you some paper to write on." He placed a pile of lined paper on my desk.

What was it with these people? Why couldn't they just leave me alone? "Get out!" I yelled and threw my pillow at him. He caught it and placed it on my desk, then left. I heard him stop outside my door and wait, making sure I didn't freak out again.

Just before supper, one of the staff took some of the girls down to the smoking room. Even though I didn't have any smokes, I went with them — second-hand smoke is better than none. When we got to the smoking room I stood around, not knowing who to talk to. Chris had stayed in the unit to finish some homework.

"Hey, Kelly." It was Pit Bull, sitting with another girl, playing cards. "Come over here," she said.

I looked at her for a moment, thinking about it. This was the first time she'd spoken to me since she'd apologized to the office wall. Why the sudden interest?

"C'mon, Kelly." Pit Bull sounded friendly enough. She could fake a believable smile when she wanted to. And who cared if her smile was real or not? Nothing about Pit Bull was real; everyone knew that. If she decided to make me one of her fake friends, I'd have it made. No one would laugh at me. When I was out of smokes, someone would give me one. No one said no to Pit Bull and her friends.

I went over and sat down. *Careful*, I thought.

"Want a smoke?" Pit Bull asked, her smile as careful as mine.

"Sure," I said. She handed me one, then held her lighter for me. I took a long deep drag. "Wish I could quit," I said.

"Don't we all. Waste of money," Pit Bull agreed. We played a hand of gin rummy while I wondered what this was about. Then Pit Bull glanced around, looking for staff, and said, "Walk down to Bingo with us tonight." There was a look in her eyes that made it an order. I waited before I answered, just so she would know that I wasn't one of her slaves.

"Okay," I said slowly.

Pit Bull smiled and said, "Good girl." Then she and the other girl got up and left the table.

She made her point, I thought. *Kelly New Girl does what she's told, just like everyone else.*

Still, when Pit Bull started joking around with me after supper chores, I had to smile. She could be funny, though most of her jokes put the other girls down. I walked with her through the long hall to the schoolroom where the weekly Bingo game was held. I could feel the other girls' eyes on me, wondering if I'd made it into Pit Bull's special circle. When we got to the Bingo room, Pit Bull kicked some girls away from the table she wanted. She always got her own private table.

"C'mon, Kelly," she said. Feeling like her pet poodle, I sat down beside her. To my relief, Fran pulled up a chair and sat with us for part of the evening. When she left, Pit Bull leaned forward.

"Thursday night after gym, I'm going to run for it," she said. "You're going to be my decoy."

I knew better than to show surprise. Keeping my face blank, I stared at my Bingo card. So this was what I was supposed to do for her. *Which door?* I thought. *How can I get her to tell me which door?*

"Sure," I said, trying to keep cool. "What d'you want me to do?"

"Just keep talking to Fran on the way back from gym," said Pit Bull. "I checked the staff schedule and she's working. That should give me all the time I need."

I took a deep breath and asked, "So, how are you going to get out?"

A slow grin crawled across Pit Bull's face. "Someday, maybe I'll send you a postcard and tell you. I'll owe you one, Kelly."

Yeah, sure, I thought. *You'll be gone and I'll be stuck here forever*. My thoughts raced around the inside of my head. Maybe she already had a key. If she did, I could steal it from her, and then I'd be the one skipping free.

"If you tell," Pit Bull said, ditching her smile, "I'll make you pay for it."

I almost laughed. Who would I tell? "What are you going to do out there?" I asked.

"I've got friends," she said.

I had to try again. Keeping the hope off my face, I repeated, "How are you getting out?"

She laughed. "You'll find out after I'm gone. I'm out of this place, man."

All I could do was stare at her face and wish I was her.

Chapter Six

Over the next few days, Pit Bull and I didn't talk to each other so that no one would suspect. I stayed in my room and started writing a story about Chris as a little kid. It made me think about my sister Jolyn, and I wanted to talk to her more than ever. Maybe if I got out of here, I could visit her in secret, without my mom knowing. As I wrote, the story-girl Chris turned into Jolyn. It was almost like talking to her, and the words poured out of me. That evening and the next I wrote every chance I got. Thursday evening I took the story with me when I went to skating.

In the long hall, Pit Bull looked at me as she walked by. I nodded. I skated by myself and thought about my decoy plan. I wondered how Pit Bull planned to get out, but I knew better than to ask again. If I tried to follow her, we might both get caught. Then she would make me pay for every breath I took in this place. And even if I escaped with her, she would probably set her friends on me for disobeying her. The best thing to hope for was that she would actually manage to escape. Then she would be gone and I could concentrate on getting out my own way.

When skating finished, I stopped Fran in the equipment room and handed her my story. She smiled and said she'd look at it when we got upstairs to the unit. But that wouldn't help Pit Bull, so I took the story back and started reading it out loud. I guess it got her attention because she walked back with me, listening the whole way. When we got up to the unit, I couldn't see Pit Bull anywhere. Still, she might need more time, so I kept talking to Fran while the other girls sat down for a snack. We went into the office.

"You're a good storyteller," Fran said. "Do you ever write about yourself?"

"Yeah, I've written lots of stories. They're in my room." The words were out of my mouth before I knew it, and I bit my lip. I had to be more careful — I didn't want the staff to know about that stuff.

"What are they about?" asked Fran.

"Oh, stuff," I said, shrugging. "My life, I guess." While I was talking, I kept checking for Pit Bull. I didn't see her anywhere.

"That's a good idea," said Fran.

"Yeah, I guess," I muttered. "I don't have that much to say."

Fran was being nice, and I was getting nervous. I had to keep her attention until I was sure that Pit Bull was gone. But you have to watch it when people are nice. They make you relax. Then you let your guard down, and they get stuff out of you.

"It doesn't have a title yet," I said, trying to change the subject. "First thing you do if you're going to write a book is give it a title — if you want to finish the book, I mean. If you're really serious, it's got a title. That way, it's for real. That way, you have to finish."

Fran was looking at me closely. "Finish what, Kelly — your book or your life?"

I stared at her. How had we started talking about this? I didn't want to talk about this sort of stuff. In my head I could see Pit Bull running down the street, getting away. My legs got all tight, I wanted to run so much.

"You're not happy here, are you?" Fran asked.

"Is anybody?" I said.

"Where would you like to be?" she asked.

"In some wide open place." I could see a huge field in the country, with no fences.

"What would you do there?" Fran asked.

"I'd run," I said right away. "I'd run and run. I used to be on the track-and-field team at my old school."

"What would you do when you got tired?" she asked.

"I'd never get tired," I said.

"Everybody gets tired sometime," she said.

"I never get tired of wanting to run," I said.

"Yeah, but as long as you're running, whatever you're running from is right behind you," Fran said.

I could feel my dad swell up inside of me.

My hands went to fists and I closed my eyes.

"What are you running from, Kelly?" Fran asked softly.

The answer was out of me before I knew it. "Me," I said. "I'm running from me. I hate myself. I hate my life. I just want to get away from myself."

"But you can't," Fran said.

Her answer came at me so hard, I felt as if I'd been hit. I opened my eyes and stared at her. This conversation had been going along so nice and easy. Why had she suddenly turned mean on me?

Fran just sat there, looking me in the eye. "That's the only thing you can't run from, Kelly. You can never run from yourself."

"Sure I can," I said, pulling up my sleeve and pointing at the bandage.

"Suicide isn't the answer, Kelly," Fran said, leaning towards me. "Suicide means the person who hurt you won. Even though that person isn't around you right now, he's still running your life. In fact, you're doing his job for him by hurting yourself." She looked at me for a moment. Then she said, "Who owns your life, Kelly? Who owns Kelly Paddik?"

"He's dead," I muttered.

"Who is?" asked Fran.

"Ah, nothing." I hadn't meant for any of this to come out. A long time ago I'd tried talking to my mom, and that had made things worse. Life happens the way it happens and you can't change that. "You don't do life," I said. "Life does you."

"You can write your life any way you want, Kelly," Fran said. "It's still all there ahead of you. Right now it's a bunch of blank pages. Suicide means you leave them blank."

"Fran." Suddenly Sister Mary was standing in the office doorway. "I need to talk to you," she said.

One look at Sister Mary's face and I knew they'd found out about Pit Bull.

"I'm going to have a snack," I said and walked away. I sat down and picked up an apple. From where I was seated, I could see Fran on the office phone, probably calling the police. I wondered how far Pit Bull had gotten. *Which door?* I kept asking myself. *How did she get out of this place?*

As I bit into the apple, Fran's words kept running through my head. She was right — someone else was running my life. My dad, of course. He was still hanging around in my head, even though he was dead. But how was I supposed to fight a ghost? I'd been trying for years, and nothing had worked.

In my room I saw the poster that Sister Mary had given me. I unrolled it. The picture wasn't that bad, really. If I folded the words LOVE YOURSELF under at the bottom, I wouldn't have to look at them. Maybe I couldn't get out of this place, but I could still pretend that I was out. From now on, whenever I started thinking about my dad, I'd pretend that I was a small white bird. Then I would up and fly away.

Chapter Seven

The next morning it looked as if nobody had figured out the part I'd played in Pit Bull's escape. Rumor had it that she'd broken out through a skylight in the social workers' area. Not that it helped much to know that *now*. That skylight would be guarded by nuns on a mission around the clock.

At midmorning break, Chris came up to me. "Want to get out of class?" she asked. "Sister Mary said I could get someone to help me do something."

"Do what?" I asked.

"Decorate the gym for Parents' Night."

I stared at her. "Parents' Night?"

"Yeah," she said. "Next Thursday. People come in and take a tour — family, or just people from the neighborhood. I'm going to be one of the tour guides."

I couldn't believe it — this place was like a jail. "What'll they think when they see the locked doors and the wire through the windows?"

"I dunno," shrugged Chris. "It's not that bad. And it's better for them to see the way it really is than to make up stories about it in their heads. So, d'you want to help?"

"Sure," I said. Anything to get out of class.

Some of the nuns and several girls were setting up tables on one side of the gym. Sister Mary set us to work cleaning up the equipment room. Then we helped her drag a ladder over to one of the gym walls. Hands on her hips, Sister Mary eyed that wall as if she was going to turn it into a work of art. Standing beside her, I couldn't believe how short she was. I was taller than her when I was ten years old. I couldn't help grinning.

Glancing up at me, Sister Mary got a stern look on her face. "Don't think you can use me as an armrest, or we'll never be friends, Kelly Paddik," she said.

Chris hooted with laughter. Without missing a beat, Sister Mary said, "You hold the ladder, Chris. Kelly, why don't you pass the banner up to me?" She started to climb without waiting for Chris to grab hold of the ladder. *This nun doesn't wait for anyone*, I thought.

I went over to the banner and read the words as I picked it up: ONE PERSON IS WORTH MORE THAN THE WHOLE WORLD. *Yeah, right*, I thought. *If they think I'm worth something, why lock me away like this?*

Sister Mary was perched on top of the ladder, staring at a spot on the wall. "I think we'll put it right here," she muttered to herself. She looked down at me and grinned. "Ready, kiddo?" she asked. As she bent forward, the ladder creaked loudly. Chris gripped it tighter and made a face.

I held up one corner of the banner. "Maybe I should get on the ladder?" I said.

"Think I'm too old for this, young lady?" Sister Mary demanded. Her glasses made her eyes look huge. Taking one corner of the banner from my hand, she started to fasten it to the wall. Suddenly there was a loud crash on the other side of the gym. We all jumped. I turned quickly to see that one of the tables had fallen over. Chris whirled too, jerking the ladder so that it wobbled. Sister Mary dropped the banner and grabbed for the top rung. She missed and began to fall backward. Jumping towards her, I tried to catch her as she fell. She landed on my shoulder and we went down together.

I knew I was okay — maybe a bruised hip. I could feel Sister Mary on top of me, her head on my shoulder. *She didn't hit her head*, I thought. Then I saw she'd twisted her leg under herself. It looked like a bad sprain. I made sure I didn't move an inch, even though my hip ached — it might have hurt Sister Mary's leg.

Then I saw the set of keys lying between my knees and the wall. *Sister Mary's!* I thought. I grabbed them and slid them into my pocket just as several nuns ran over. I told them that I was fine, and they held Sister Mary carefully as I got up. Putting my hands in my pockets, I stood quietly beside Chris as they checked Sister Mary's leg. I couldn't believe that I was holding a set of keys to this place. The keys in my hand felt as if they had wings. I held them tightly. *Don't fly away yet*, I thought.

Sister Mary's face was pulled into a very old shape, full of pain. "I'll get a car and we'll take you to the hospital," said another nun, bending over her.

"No," snapped Sister Mary angrily. She meant what she'd said. I couldn't believe it — her leg was starting to turn color and swell up.

"Mary, this is no time for being a hero. You have to go," the other nun told her.

"I'm not seeing a doctor," said Sister Mary. "Just help me up to my room. No one's going to touch this leg."

One of the nuns sent everyone back to class. I walked beside Chris down the hall, holding the secret keys in my pocket. Finally I had my chance to get out of this place. All I had to do was find a time when nobody was watching me. It wouldn't work while I was at the school. There were too many people all over the place.

"Do you think it was our fault?" Chris looked worried. "They won't think we did it on purpose, will they?"

"No," I shrugged. It was just Sister Mary's leg, not her heart, and I had more important things to think about. "Don't worry about it," I said. "See you later."

As I walked away from Chris, I had to work to keep the smile off my face. This bird was going to fly the coop, really soon.

Chapter Eight

I'd decided to hide the keys in the heating vent in my room, but then I got a better idea. After school, I taped the most important key inside the folded part of the poster. Then I dropped the rest into the garbage pail in the girls' washroom. When I came out, I noticed Jim talking to Chris in the office. She kept shaking her head. I guessed that Sister Mary had finally noticed that her keys were missing. Jim called me into the office and asked if I'd seen them. I just kept saying no. It was pretty obvious that he didn't believe me, but he couldn't force me to say anything.

The staff did a room search. I had to watch from my doorway as Jim went through all my stuff a second time. He looked in the heating vent, under my bed and through my closet. But he didn't think of checking behind the poster. So when he walked out of my room, I still had the key.

After an hour or so the staff stopped searching the other girls' rooms. I wondered if they'd found the keys I'd thrown into the washroom garbage, but they didn't say anything. If they had found them, they would have noticed that the master key was gone. Maybe that was why they kept their eyes on me like spotlights. I don't know why, but they just seemed to know that Chris hadn't taken the keys. With the staff watching me like that, there wasn't a single chance to make a break for it. Every time I moved off on my own, a staff would call out, "Kelly, come watch this TV show." Or someone would say, "Kelly, come play pool with us."

That night they brought in extra staff. After lights out I lay awake for hours, waiting for a chance to slip out. But every time I checked, I could see a woman sitting in the middle of the unit. She wasn't watching TV the way the night staff usually did. Her eyes kept moving from one bedroom door to the next, waiting for someone to come out. And she didn't look as if she'd go for the "I have to use the washroom" excuse. Several times she actually came over to my room and shone a flashlight on me. I did my best to fake sleep. At one point she even sat outside my door for awhile. It was creepy, and I didn't fall asleep until she moved back to the middle of the unit.

The next morning the key was still hidden inside the poster. It was Saturday, and after breakfast Chris decided to teach me how to bake bannock. As we got out the flour and eggs, I kept thinking about the key. Saturday was usually a quiet day — maybe I'd get my chance to take off. So far I'd only noticed one extra staff working.

But as we finished mixing up the bannock, we saw Jim walk Pit Bull across the unit to her room. My jaw dropped. I'd thought for sure she would made it. Pit Bull was tough, and she'd said she had friends out there. What had happened to them? And what had happened to *her*? She looked as if she'd been sleeping in the dump, and her clothes were torn. When she came out of her room with a towel, I saw her black eye. As she walked past us, she didn't look up. I glanced at Chris to see what she thought, and she just shrugged.

"Terri's always going on the run," she said coolly. "She usually comes back looking like a wreck."

Pit Bull stayed in the tub room for a long time. When she got out, the staff didn't let her go back to her room. Instead she had to stay in the back room, a small locked room behind the office. All that room had in it was a bed and a window with wires running through it. After a while, Pit Bull started to kick and punch the walls. The sounds reminded me of my dad when he got angry. I went stiff, and my hands started to shake.

"Pit Bull's flipping out," I whispered.

Chris shrugged again. "So what else is new? She always ends up in the back room, kicking in another wall. She thinks she's a big shot, but she's never going to change. Terri will be in here forever. I'm going to get my life straight so I can get out of here for good."

After we finished the bannock, I played gin rummy with some girls but I couldn't sit still. I kept walking around the unit, looking out the windows. Every time I looked at the office, I could see Jim watching me. Pit Bull's banging got louder and louder, but I figured a staff must be in the back room with her. It sounded as if there might be a restraint. Everyone hates it when a girl loses it and has to be restrained. The staff hold her down until she stops fighting.

Suddenly we heard a beautiful voice singing its way up the stairs, along with some loud thumping. "Sister Mary!" someone called. The rest of the girls crowded into the hall beside the office, but I hung back. What if Sister Mary figured out that I'd taken her keys? Would she think I'd jiggled the ladder so that she would fall off and I could steal them? I kept thinking of her looking up at me and saying, "Don't think you can use me as an armrest." She was such a cool old lady, she probably *knew*. When she turned into the unit, I almost ran for my room. Her leg was all bandaged up and she was on crutches.

"Hello, ladies!" She looked past the rest of the girls and smiled at me. "Thanks for trying to catch me when I fell, Kelly," she said.

"Yeah, sure," I muttered. My eyes looked everywhere but at her face.

"Did you go to the doctor?" Chris asked.

"No," said Sister Mary, "but I did drag myself to the nurse. She says I'll live. Now, ladies, if you'll excuse me, I have to have a word with Terri."

Slowly Sister Mary turned herself on her crutches and hobbled into the back room. I couldn't believe she was going in there. Pit Bull was rabid.

"What's she going to do if Pit Bull goes for her?" I asked Chris nervously.

All the girls stood around stiff, listening. Everyone liked Sister Mary, with her old big band songs and jokes. We could hear her in the back room, talking to Pit Bull, her voice calm and steady. Everything seemed okay, but if that nun cried out, there were eight girls waiting to save her. I stood with the others, my arms and legs tense and ready to move. I knew how angry a girl could get. When I got really mad, I didn't think. Sometimes I lost it, and then I thought anyone near me was my dad coming to get me again. I would fight to save myself, and when I was like that I could hurt anyone around me.

None of the girls said anything, but I figured everyone was thinking pretty much the same thing. The funny thing was that after a while, Pit Bull got quieter. She stopped banging and yelling, and we heard her start talking to Sister Mary. Then she started to cry. I don't know why, but when I heard Pit Bull crying, tears stung my own eyes. I guess I'd never thought of her as someone who *could* cry. She sounded like a little kid, like my sister Jolyn.

Jim came out of the office and smiled at us. "Are any of you mother hens interested in going out to the yard?"

Chris and I went down the back stairs with him and waited as he unlocked the door at the bottom. For the first time in weeks, I stepped outside. It had gotten colder, and I was glad that Chris had made me wear a jacket. We sat on a bench, smoking and looking around. Jim sat nearby. I kept taking quick glances at the fence. It wasn't far off, and it looked easy to climb. I was just waiting for Jim to take his eyes off me. No one said much. In my head I could still hear Sister Mary's voice, talking quietly to Pit Bull.

"Why is Sister Mary afraid to see a doctor?" I asked Chris. "She won't see a doctor, but she'll walk into a back room with Pit Bull flipping out? I wouldn't go in there for anything."

"Why won't you talk to Jim?" Chris asked.

I glared at her. Chris looked right back, though her eyes looked a little scared. She knew I wanted to punch her out for asking me that. People from Churchill have a lot of guts.

"Jim won't hurt you," Chris said. "Social workers are here to help, y'know. I talk to him lots."

Suddenly all I could see was the wall in Jim's office turning into my dad's face. "Never," I snapped. Jumping up, I took off for the fence. It was just a chain-link fence, easy to climb. I could see the street through it, the dead leaves blowing past. It would take no more than a second to climb, less than a second. My fingers grabbed for the fence, and I got one foot into the mesh, ready to swing myself up. But then a hand grabbed my arm, and Jim shoved me against the fence. I wanted to scream and push him off, but I stayed quiet. My whole body was like a hand, hanging onto that fence.

"Let's go back in, Kelly," Jim said. "It's time to go in."

"Yeah, sure." I didn't look at him or Chris. "Anything you say. Anything at all."

Chapter Nine

I had to stay in my room all afternoon, and a staff checked me every ten minutes. I think I would have been put in the back room, but Pit Bull was already there. So I sat staring at the white bird on my poster and thinking my thoughts. At three o'clock, Fran came on shift. She didn't say much, just looked in on me every ten minutes. The afternoon felt as heavy as the gray sky outside my window. Dead leaf after dead leaf blew past.

I joined the group for supper, then was sent back to my room. I could hear the rest of the girls sitting down to watch a video. Then Fran knocked on my door.

"Chris and I are going downstairs to play pool," she said. "Want to come?"

Chris didn't turn out to be the world's best pool player. Sometimes she would cross her eyes, then take her shot. Fran seemed to be aiming at the ceiling or, better yet, the window. When I played pool, even with good friends, I played to win. But it was hard with Chris laughing and Fran whooping every time she shot a ball onto the floor. I rolled my eyes and went to get a ball that Fran had knocked behind the sofa.

"So, Chris, tomorrow's the big day, eh?" Fran said.

"What's that?" I fished the pool ball out of some dust and stood up.

"I get my outings," Chris told me. "I get to go for a walk outside by myself — a whole twenty minutes without staff around to bug me." Chris shot Fran a grin. "Jim said that if I handle these walks by myself, I'll be able to move to a group home."

I listened for the lie in her voice, but Chris

didn't sound as if she planned to run. "On top of all that, I'm quitting smoking," she added grandly. "For the third time this month. Of course, I quit every time I finish a pack." She sighed. "I want to save up and buy a horse."

"Where are you going to keep it?" I asked. "Can't keep a horse in a group home."

"I dunno," Chris giggled. "I've always wanted to get a horse and call it Truck."

Fran chuckled. "Giddyap, Truck! Whoa, Truck!"

I thought they were both very weird. I was trying to show Chris how to get her next shot right when the phone rang. Fran picked it up and listened. Right away she ditched her smile.

"Okay. We'll be right up." She hung up the phone. "Sorry, ladies, but we have to head back upstairs. Maybe we can finish this heavy-duty game later, eh?"

At the top of the stairs we saw another staff waiting for us. Next to her stood Pit Bull, one arm wrapped in a tea towel and pressed against her stomach. Blood had soaked through the towel onto her shirt. She stared at her feet and ignored us.

"See you later," Fran said as we passed them.

They must be going to the hospital, I thought.

When we got back to the unit, Chris and I went into my room. I flopped onto my bed and stared at the ceiling. Chris sat on the floor, her back against the wall. I couldn't believe that Pit Bull had slashed her arm. Even if she'd surprised me by crying, I still couldn't believe she would slash her arm. If there was anyone in this unit who had everything under control, it was Pit Bull. She controlled everything and everyone within breathing distance. But slashing meant you'd lost it — you were out of control. Believe me, I knew that. It was only a few days now until my stitches were supposed to come out.

"I can't believe she did that," I said.

"Why not?" asked Chris.

"She's always so tough," I said. "She laughed when she saw my arm." I looked at Chris. "You ever slash?" I asked her.

Chris rubbed her forehead. "I thought about it a couple of times. But I guess Fran changed my mind."

"How'd she do that?" I asked.

"Well, she knows about what my father did to me." Chris's face got very pale and twisted around when she said this. "He ... sexually abused me. I don't really like to talk about it. I still get nightmares sometimes. I did a lot of dumb junk to forget."

"The usual?" I asked. I knew what that meant — drugs, drinking, AWOLs, hooking.

Chris kept twisting her hands. "Sometimes ... well, I still can't forget and I get hyper." I thought she might start to cry, but she swallowed and went on. "They put me in a group home because I kept running away. As long as I saw an open door, I was out and gone. I know my dad wasn't hurting me anymore. All that ... sexual abuse ... was over, but I kept thinking about it. I'd think about it every time I had to stay in one place. I had to keep moving. I just looked for an open door and took off."

I was watching her face closely. It was like hearing my own story, except that my dad died in a car crash a few years ago. I thought I'd be rid of him then, but he was still here, hanging around inside my head.

Chris sighed. "I kept taking off until they put me in here. Then I couldn't run anymore." She started scratching the back of her hand — not deep, just nervous. I knew what that meant

— not scared enough to slash, but thinking about it. "Y'know how when you run," Chris said, "you feel like you're getting out ... I dunno ... of the mess inside you?"

I nodded.

"That's why I always ran," she said. "But with these walls, there's no place to go. I did a lot of kicking and yelling when I first got here. Then Fran told me that it was really my dad who was doing the kicking and yelling. He wanted to hurt me, and I was still letting him do that to me."

She must say that to everyone, I thought.

"Well, I thought about it and I figured she was right," Chris said. "Why should I wreck my life? If I worked it all out and did okay, he'd be more surprised than anybody."

"So what did you do?" I asked. "You seem okay now."

"Well, this sounds stupid," Chris said, "but I just talked about it. I talked to Fran and then to Jim. A lot of kids talk to them. Jim's heard a lot of that stuff. He listens and asks questions. Someday I'm going to be a social worker like Jim, but up in Churchill."

Slowly I pulled up my sleeve and looked at

the stitches on my arm. "I thought this would be the end of it all, y'know?" I said.

"Guess you're stuck with being alive longer than you thought," Chris said softly.

"I guess," I muttered. I thought about Pit Bull, her arm wrapped in a tea towel, not looking at us. I didn't want to turn out like her. But the idea of talking to Jim scared me. What if talking about my dad made him show up in my head again?

"You should give the key back," Chris said suddenly.

A wave of shock washed over me. I glanced quickly at Chris, then away, so she wouldn't see the surprise in my eyes. "I don't have any keys," I said.

"Yes, you do," Chris said.

"Yeah?" I demanded. "Where are they?"

Chris pulled the set of keys I'd thrown into the washroom garbage out of her pocket. "Guess where I found these," she said. "But the master key is gone. You've got it."

"Prove it." I sat up, my heart pounding. I had to keep that key. It was my only chance to get out of this place.

Chris just sat there and looked at me,

swinging the keys around her finger.

"What are you going to do with those, Chris?" I asked.

She looked at the keys for a moment. "Oh, I might say that I found them at school in the gym," she said. "Or I might say that I found them in the garbage in the washroom in the unit. I haven't made up my mind. What are you going to do with your key?"

Lie after lie floated through my head, but I decided to say nothing. "This doesn't have anything to do with me," I said, turning my back. "You do what you want, Chris. Just leave me out of it, okay?"

Chapter Ten

That night I lay in bed, pinching myself to stay awake. I was wearing sweats over my pajamas, and I felt thick and lumpy. After that talk with Chris, I figured I had to make my break right away. The staff who worked nights always stayed awake, but sometimes they left the unit. And for some reason the extra staff who'd worked last night was gone. I listened to the night staff moving around. When I heard her leave the unit, I peered through my doorway. There was no one in sight — the staff must be checking on Pit Bull in the back room.

I slid the key out of the folded section of the poster. Then I snuck through the unit and out the back door. The stairway was very dark, lit only by EXIT signs. At the bottom of the stairs I dropped the key. It hit my foot so there wasn't much noise, but I had to get down on my knees to find it.

My body felt full of strange whispering voices, and I kept looking over my shoulder. It felt as if someone was coming down the stairs towards me, someone I couldn't hear but I knew he was there. *Come on, come on*, hissed a voice in my head. *You've got to get away or you know what will happen.*

Finally my hand bumped against the key. I grabbed it, stood up and tried to fit it into the lock. I was so nervous that it took a couple of tries to get it into the keyhole. That feeling of someone coming towards me was growing, as if he was right behind me.

After what seemed like forever, I felt the key slide into the lock. I tried to turn it, but the key wouldn't move. I tried again, jamming it hard. The key still didn't move. I knew this was the right key — I'd watched so many staff lock and unlock doors with it.

Then it hit me — they'd changed the locks. I'd waited too long, and now there was nowhere to run. In the dark, with all those EXIT signs around me, I backed against the door. I knew who was coming for me — someone bigger than real life, scarier. Suddenly my dad was there again, in the dark all around me. I couldn't move. I was gripping the key so tightly it cut into my hand.

I can't do this alone, I thought. *He's bigger than me.*

After a long time under the EXIT sign I climbed back up the stairs. I waited until I saw the night staff go into the washroom. Then I climbed into bed and slipped the key under my pillow.

Chapter Eleven

The next afternoon, Chris pulled on her jacket and left to go on her big twenty-minute walk. I sat in the kitchen, playing cards and watching the clock. Some of the girls held a countdown. Even I wasn't sure if she would come back. And the strange thing was that I wanted her to — I wanted to believe that she meant what she said. I wanted to believe someone could straighten out in here.

She was a few minutes late, but that was

because a staff had to go down to let her in. Chris came over to my table, trying to ignore the fact that everyone was staring at her.

"Weather's nice out today," she grinned.

"We can see out the window," snapped Pit Bull. She was back from the hospital, sitting in front of the TV, her bandaged arm across her stomach. We ignored her. Chris said that she'd gone to the McDonald's at the corner and ordered a Sprite.

"Why'd you come back?" someone asked.

"I don't want to get out of here for a couple of days." Chris sounded scornful. "When I go, I'm leaving here for good." Fran walked by and Chris added loudly, with a grin, "Just so none of these staff can ever bug me again."

"Ever sick, Chris," Fran winked.

The next day I asked to see Jim. I was pretty nervous walking into his office. I felt as if he already knew everything that I was going to tell him — as if he could read my mind. I laid Sister Mary's key on his desk. "I tried this and it didn't work," I said. "When did you change the locks?"

He looked surprised, which made me feel better. I didn't know how to get started, so I said that Chris's story about her dad sounded a lot like mine. This was hard to say. Even that little bit made me think I saw my dad out of the corner of my eye. But I had to keep going. I held onto the arms of my chair to help myself remember where I was. *It's over*, I thought. *It's not happening now*. Sometimes I could feel myself crying, and I stared out of the office window while I talked.

I didn't tell Jim everything that day, but it was a start. He did ask some pretty good questions. Sometimes they made me remember things I didn't want to think about. If they hit too close, I didn't answer them. Not yet.

"Would you like to tell your mother how angry you are at her?" asked Jim. He said he knew that my mom hadn't tried to stop the abuse. Just as I'd thought, he already knew my secret. But not because he could read my mind — my mom had told him.

"She won't listen," I said. "She never listened to me before."

"Your mother has been seeing a counselor for a year now," Jim told me. "She's been working pretty hard. Why don't you try to talk to her? I'll be here with you."

"I'll think about it," I said.

I did think about it — all afternoon and evening. Before I went to bed I asked Fran to let Jim know that I'd decided to talk to my mom. Then I knocked on Chris's door. She was sitting on her bed, reading a comic and chewing on a pen. There were ink marks all over her face. I was pretty sure she didn't know that they were there.

"I just wanted to tell you that I gave Jim the key," I said.

"Yeah?" She grinned. There was ink on her teeth.

"Yeah," I said. "I talked to him today. He's okay."

"I dropped the key ring on the gym teacher's desk," Chris said. "I heard her tell someone she found it."

I nodded. "Thanks for trying to cover for me, but they know I took them now."

"Okay." She shrugged and grinned.

"Do you know you have ink all over your face?" I asked.

"Do I?" Chris shrieked and ran for the washroom.

Wednesday after school I sat in Jim's office

scratching softly at my arms. Jim was talking about something, but I could hardly listen. There came a knock on the door. My mom walked in.

"Hello, Mrs. Paddik," Jim said, standing up.

I felt a huge hole open in my stomach. I hadn't seen my mom for four years. There was a lot of gray in her hair and new lines in her face. For a second I wanted to touch her, just to make sure she was real.

"Hello, Kelly." She sat down slowly in the chair next to me.

"Hi." I looked away. What was I supposed to say to her?

Somehow Jim got us talking. What really surprised me was that my mom listened to most of what I said, even when I yelled. A few times I saw tears in her eyes, and then I had to stop. Crying really gets to me, I guess. Even when I still thought that I hated my mom, I didn't want to make her cry.

She said she was sorry and that it was her fault that I was in trouble. "It's because I've been seeing a counselor that I can say these things to you," she told me. "Before, I knew you were right, but I felt too guilty. Your father ... hurt me too, and that's why I wasn't able to help you."

Well, I knew what it was like to hurt too much to care about anyone else. I nodded. Then she told me that Jolyn and Danny were doing okay and living with her.

I could tell Jim was pretty pleased with our meeting. He invited my mom to come back the next day for Parents' Night. I couldn't believe my mom had said what she'd said. And I couldn't believe some of the things that I'd yelled at her — or that she'd listened.

It was as if all those things that I'd never talked about had taken up space inside me, swelling up when I got angry. But as I talked to my mom, the memories started to leave me through my mouth. I still remembered what happened, but now it felt like for the first time the memories were outside my body, leaving space inside for me. I felt as if I could be more than what my dad had done to me. I didn't know what that was, but I sure wanted to find out.

Later that day I sat in my room, looking at the poster Sister Mary had given me. Standing up, I went over and folded the words back out so that I could see them. LOVE YOURSELF. Ideas for stories floated slowly through my head. *Love yourself*, I wrote on a piece of paper. Then I wrote, *Love who? Who are you? Kelly. Who is Kelly? Who owns Kelly Paddik?*

I thought a minute. Then I wrote, *I want to*.

A little later I went out to play cards with Chris, but she was out on another one of her walks. This time, though, I wasn't worried. I finally understood why she was going to come back.

Chapter Twelve

Months later I sat in that same bedroom, staring out of the same window. The yellow leaves were gone and the tree branches were lined with snow and ice. For four months I'd been talking to Jim, Fran and my mom. Believe me, it was a lot better than talking to my pet rock. My mom brought Jolyn and Danny to visit me every Sunday, and we talked lots on the phone. In a couple of weeks I would be starting home visits on weekends. Then in the summer, if everything went well, I would get to move back home.

I'd also been writing down everything that happened to me. I was sitting at my desk and in my hands I held my whole life, in words, on paper. I had written down everything I could remember. Now it was outside of me. I could hold it in my hands, put it in a drawer, even throw it away if I wanted to. It wasn't hiding inside me anymore, taking up space. I'd gotten it all out.

"Hey, Kelly." It was Chris, standing in my doorway. Next week she was moving out of the unit to a group home.

"What?" I asked.

"Can you believe it?" Chris laughed. "Terri wants me to help her hold up Fran. She says she stole a fork and she's got it in her room. She wants to hold it to Fran's throat and get her keys. D'you think she'll ever change? I told her to fork off."

I had to laugh. "You're crazy. C'mon in and listen to a story I just finished writing. I have to figure out a title for it."

Chris flopped onto my bed and picked up my stuffed bear. "Who gave you this polar bear, anyway?" she asked.

I swallowed and looked down. "My dad, when I was real little. I don't remember anything nice about him besides that bear."

Chris turned the bear around in her hands. "Keep it then," she said softly. "Now, read me your story."

"Okay." I picked up the last page. I hadn't shown it to anyone yet. Suddenly I got so nervous, my voice ran away on me. I kept clearing my throat, trying to get it to come back.

"I can't hear you," Chris said loudly. "You're whispering."

"Oh," I whispered. "Sorry."

"Start over," said Chris. Sometimes she could be pretty bossy. I cleared my throat again.

"Hey, Kelly." Chris's voice was wobbling, and I looked up to see what was the matter. She was twisting her hands and watching me, her brown eyes very large. "I think you could write just about the best book in the whole world," she said.

A smile took over my whole body. I started again, trying not to whisper. "I've seen lots of movies they show about teenage girls who are supposed to be like me," I said. "They're mean and tough, and they work the streets and do drugs. Well, I've done those things, and in real life it isn't cool. You get beat up. You go hungry, and you're cold a lot. You do the drugs to forget what's happening, but you can't really forget. If you see a stray cat in an alley, don't kick it. It's just a street kid in another life, looking for some way to stay alive.

"I don't want to run anymore. I don't know where I thought I was running to anyway. You can't run from yourself.

"Someone important once said to me, 'Who owns Kelly Paddik?' That was a good question. I couldn't tell her then because I didn't like the answer — my dad. Well, it was my dad *then*. Now it's different. Now everything is different because it's me. I own Kelly Paddik. I do. I belong to me."

I looked out the window at the cold and the snow. "Well, that's the last page, I guess," I said.

"That's good. I think that's real good." Chris was patting my bear gently. "Have you got a title?"

I nodded slowly. "Now I do."

"What is it?" Chris asked.

I looked out the window. The sun had lit the ice on the branches so that they shone like glass. "Yeah, I know what I want to call it," I said softly.

"Okay, so you can tell me now." Chris was getting bossy again.

"*I Own Kelly Paddik.*" I wrote it across page one and looked at it. "Yeah, that's right. I do." I grinned at Chris. "Want to hear the whole thing now?" I asked.

Chris put the bear onto the floor. Then she stretched out on the bed and placed her hands behind her head. "I've got time," she grinned back at me.

I picked up page one.

orca soundings

Orca Soundings is a teen fiction series that features realistic teenage characters in stories that focus on contemporary situations and problems.

Soundings are short, thematic novels ideal for class or independent reading. Written by such stalwart authors as William Bell, Beth Goobie, Sheree Fitch and Kristin Butcher, there will be between eight and ten new titles a year.

For more information and reading copies, please call Orca Book Publishers at 1-800-210-5277.

Other titles in the Orca Soundings series: